PRINCESS POOH

KATHLEEN M. MULDOON

Illustrated by Linda Shute

Albert Whitman & Company, Niles, Illinois

To Kate and Bill Bohr, with love.
K.M.

Text © 1989 by Kathleen M. Muldoon
Illustrations © 1989 by Linda Shute
Design by Karen A. Yops

Published in 1989 by Albert Whitman & Company,
5747 West Howard Street, Niles, Illinois 60648.
Published simultaneously in Canada
by General Publishing, Limited, Toronto.
All rights reserved.
Printed in the United States of America.
10 9 8 7 6 5 4 3 2

Library of Congress Cataloging-in-Publication Data

Muldoon, Kathleen M.
Princess Pooh.

Summary: Jealous of her invalid sister's royal
treatment as she sits in her wheelchair,
Patty Jean tries out the conveyance and discovers life
in a wheelchair is no fun at all.
[1. Physically handicapped—Fiction. 2. Sisters—
Fiction] I. Shute, Linda, ill. II. Title.
PZ7.M889Pr 1989 [E] 88-33978
ISBN 0-8075-6627-6

A Note for You from the Author

Did you ever see someone rolling along in a wheelchair? Maybe you thought, "I'll bet I could drive one of those. It looks easy and fun!" That's what I used to think, too. Then one day an unusual disease made the bones in my legs so weak I couldn't stand anymore. Learning to push myself in a wheelchair, put on leg braces, and walk with crutches was much harder than it looked. The funny thing was that it was almost as hard for my family and friends to get used to the new way I did things as it was for me.

Being near a person who needs help doing everyday things can bring up all sorts of feelings. If there is a member of your family who uses a wheelchair or crutches, you might feel jealous of them or angry or scared. But if you talk to that person, touch their wheelchair, or even try it out, you might, like Patty Jean in this story, find that some of the painful feelings will start to go away.

—Kathleen M. Muldoon

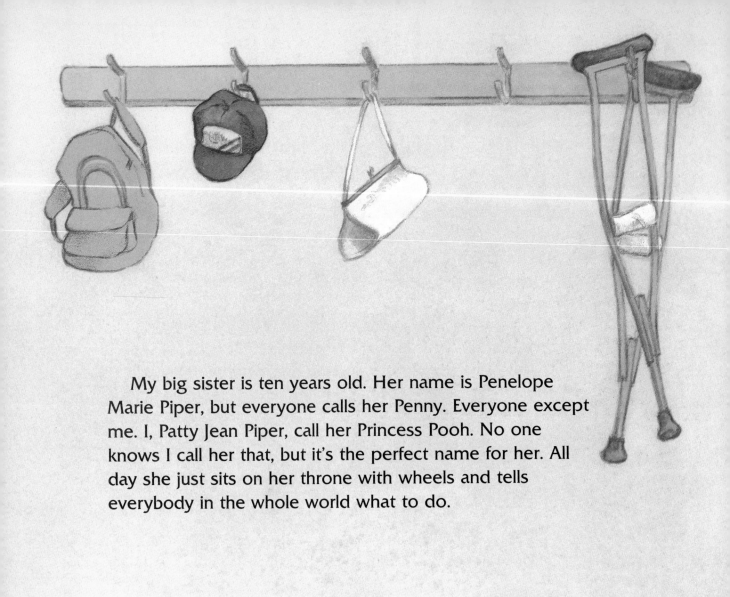

My big sister is ten years old. Her name is Penelope
Marie Piper, but everyone calls her Penny. Everyone except
me. I, Patty Jean Piper, call her Princess Pooh. No one
knows I call her that, but it's the perfect name for her. All
day she just sits on her throne with wheels and tells
everybody in the whole world what to do.

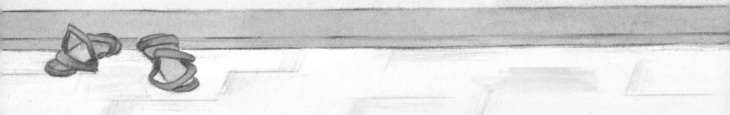

When we go shopping at the mall, Princess Pooh rides on her throne while Dad wheels her around. She smiles and waves like she's some kind of movie star. Mom carries the Princess's crutches and I, Patty Jean the Servant, carry packages. Sometimes there are so many I look like a box with legs.

Everyone loves the Princess. Grandma and Grandpop and all the aunts and uncles and cousins in our family hug her and say how sweet and wonderful she is. Then they look at me and say I am growing like a weed. That's the way it has been for a million years. The Princess is a flower. I, plain old Patty Jean, am a weed.

Once we went to a carnival. Princess Pooh watched me ride a hundred times on the roller coaster. It was fun, but it would have been better with a friend. I almost wished the Princess could ride with me. Then I tried to win a pink stuffed poodle. I spent all my allowance and threw a thousand balls, but I couldn't knock down the bottles. When we left, the man handed Princess Pooh a yellow stuffed poodle with a diamond collar! That's how it is. Everyone gives her things.

My school is a hundred years old. It is so far from my house I have to ride for hours on a school bus to get there. Princess Pooh goes to the new school right across the street. She can wheel herself there in one second.

If it rains, Dad carries her and her throne to his car and gives her a one-second ride. I, Patty Jean, wear an icky yellow raincoat and stand in mud puddles, waiting for the bus.

Saturday is chore day. Mom mows the lawn. Dad washes clothes and cleans the garage. Then he brings the clean clothes to the Princess, and she folds them into piles on the table. I, Patty Jean the Maid, clean the bathroom.

One Saturday, Mom asked me to fold clothes because Princess Pooh had therapy. I sat at the table pretending I was the Princess. I folded the clothes very fast and put them in perfect stacks. When the Princess came home, I waited for Mom to tell her to clean the bathroom. But Mom put her right to bed because she was tired. So I, exhausted Patty Jean, had to clean the bathroom, too.

It is summer now. All my friends have gone to camp—everyone except me. Mom says there's no money to send me to camp because the Princess got new braces for her legs. Princess Pooh doesn't need them anyway because all she does is sit. She only takes little tiny walks, like when she has to go to the bathroom at a restaurant and her wheelchair won't fit through the door. Mom says she walks at therapy, too, but I've never seen her do it.

After dinner I go outside. The Princess is in the hammock reading a book.

"Do you want to make a puppet show?" I ask.

"No, thanks," she says in her princess voice. "I'm going to read lots of books so I can win a prize in the summer reading program."

I don't feel like reading, but I get a book anyway and look at the pictures. I am finished in one minute.

"This book is boring," I say. "Let's play with puppets now." The Princess doesn't answer. I look over at the hammock—there she is, asleep.

Behind the tree is the throne. Seeing it empty gives me the best idea anyone in the whole world has ever had. Today I, Patty Jean, will be the Princess!

I sit on the throne. It is covered with cushions and feels like a cloud.

"I will rest on my golden throne for the whole evening," I say. I imagine all the people in my kingdom, looking at me and loving their beautiful new princess.

The throne is hard to wheel on the grass, so I get up and pull it to the front yard. "Now I will spend *every minute* on the throne," I say.

I decide to ride to the Princess's school. There is a nice, steep little hill on the grass near the sidewalk. Maybe it would be fun to ride down it. I sit down and give the throne a good, hard push.

PLOP! The throne dumps me out on the sidewalk and lands upside down on top of me. My knee has a tiny cut on it, but it doesn't hurt much. Still, I'm glad no one is around to laugh. I wonder if Princess Pooh ever fell when she was learning. I put the throne rightside up and get back on it. Then I ride to the corner. I go down the low place on the curb so I can cross the street.

When the light turns green, I push the wheels as fast as I can. I make it to the island in the middle, but then the light turns red again.

Cars and trucks and buses rush by. I cover my face so I will not see myself go SPLAT. Finally, the traffic stops and the light is green again. I finish crossing the street.

I push the throne up the low place at the crosswalk. It is
hard to go uphill, but I do it. I wheel down the sidewalk. I've
been pushing so hard I feel like both my arms are broken.
Some grown-ups are walking toward me. They look at
me and my throne, and then they turn away fast, like I do

when I'm watching a scary movie. Does this happen to Princess Pooh?

Some boys are playing on the sidewalk and will not move out of my way. "Why don't you go over me, Wheel Legs?" says one of them. All his friends laugh. "I'll beat you up!" I yell, but they just laugh some more and run away.

I see an ice-cream truck on the school playground. Lots of big kids are crowded around it. I make a shortcut across the baseball field, but by the time I get there and take some money out of my pocket, the worst thing in the world has happened. Great big raindrops have started falling over everything! SLAM goes the window on the truck. The children squeal and run away. The man drives off and I'm alone on my wet throne.

The rain comes faster and faster. I think about running home, too, but I can't leave the throne out in the rain. Besides, I am still the Princess. I'm spending every minute on my throne, even if I do get wet! So I push harder and harder. When I get back to the baseball field, I can see it's a muddy mess. The wheels of the throne sink down, down, down. They stop turning. My hands are covered with mud. I jump off the throne, and my new sandals sink, too. My feet go with them. By the time I pull the throne out, I am wetter and colder than I have ever been in my whole life. I, Princess Patty Jean, am a royal mess. It is definitely time to quit sitting on the throne.

The rain stops. Across the street there is a rainbow. I notice Dad standing in our front yard. He is calling and calling, but the cars and trucks are so noisy I can't hear him. Mom is walking up the street, looking around. I drag the muddy throne across the rest of the field to the sidewalk. Then I cross the street. When Mom sees me, she runs and holds out her arms. Dad is right behind her.

"I didn't mean to mess up the throne. I'm sorry," I say.

"Throne?" says Mom. "Oh, the *wheelchair*. We thought you were lost!"

"You weren't looking for the chair?" I say.

"Patty Jean, we were looking for *you*." Mom hugs me some more. "You shouldn't have taken Penny's chair. But we're so glad you're back!"

Mom washes me in the bathtub and puts me to bed just like she does for Penny. After Dad and Mom say good-night and turn out the lights, I lie there thinking.

"Penny," I whisper. "Are you awake?"

"Uh-huh."

"Do you like walking better than sitting?"

"Well," she says, "walking makes me awful tired, but so does pushing my wheelchair. I guess I like the wheelchair best because I can do things with my hands while I sit. When I use my crutches, I can't."

"How can you smile all the time when you're in that yucky chair?"

"It's not yucky," says Penny. "It takes me places I can't go if I just have my crutches."

That makes me think some more. "I'm sorry I took your chair," I say.

"That's all right. Just go to sleep now."

But I'm wide awake. I lie there and wish very hard that my sister will always be able to do things that make her happy. I think that maybe Princess isn't a good name for her, after all. Maybe it's nicer that she's just Penelope Marie and that I am her sister, Patty Jean Piper.